PORTVILLE FREE LIBRARY
Portville, New York 14770

DISCARDED FROM THE
PORTVILLE FREE LIBRARY

Natalie Underneath

This is Brinton's book.

Copyright © 1990 by Betsy James

All rights reserved.

Published in the United States by
Dutton Children's Books,
a division of Penguin Books USA Inc.

Published simultaneously in Canada by
Fitzhenry & Whiteside Limited, Toronto

Designer: Barbara Powderly

Printed in Hong Kong by South China Printing Co.
First Edition   10 9 8 7 6 5 4 3 2 1

Library of Congress Cataloging-in-Publication Data

James, Betsy.
    Natalie underneath/by Betsy James.
        p.   cm.
    Summary: Natalie and her brother Thomas enjoy
being underneath various things as they play.
    ISBN 0-525-44591-9
    [1. Play—Fiction. 2. Brothers and sisters—Fiction.]
I. Title.   89-23534
PZ7.J15357Nat 1990   CIP
[E]—dc20   AC

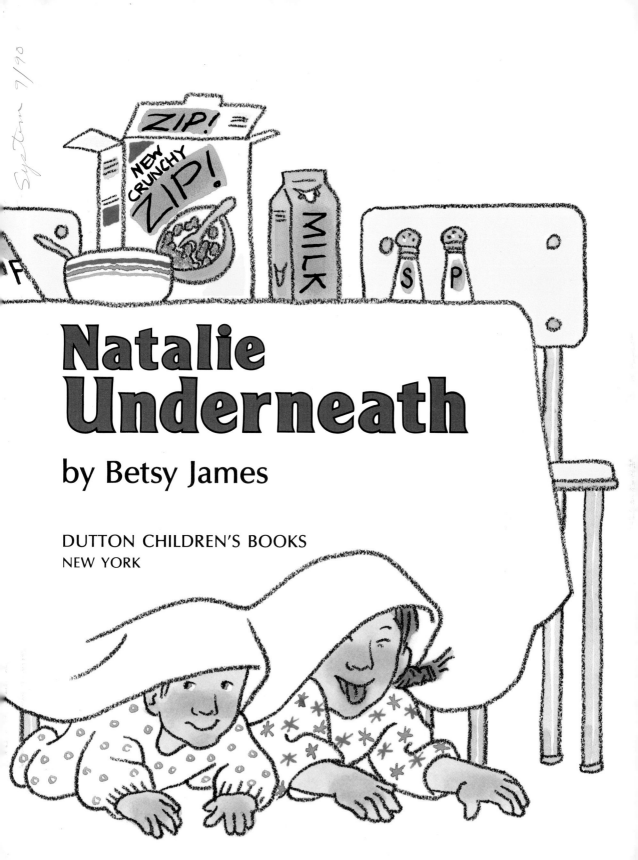

Natalie Underneath

by Betsy James

DUTTON CHILDREN'S BOOKS
NEW YORK

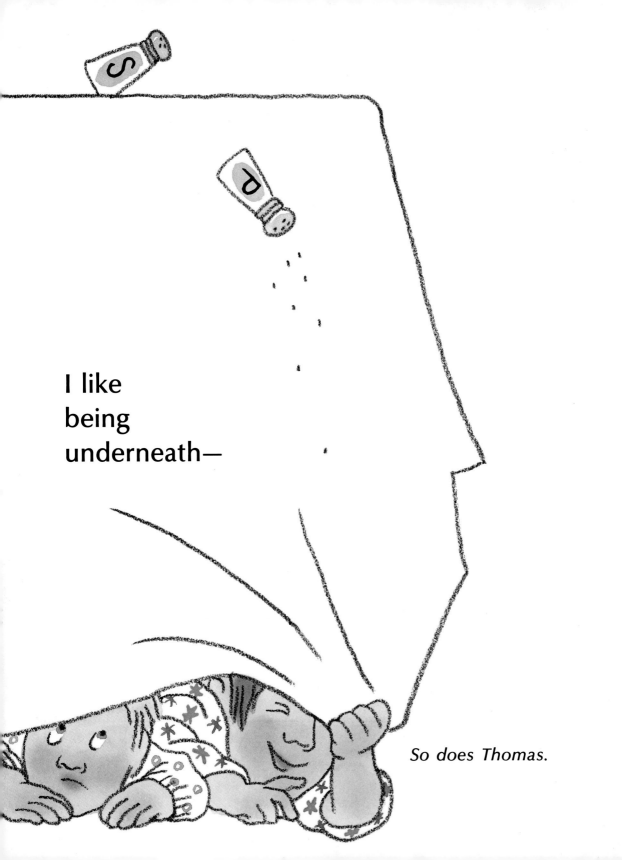

I like
being
underneath—

So does Thomas.

under the tablecloth,
playing bears,

under the chairs,

and under
the newspaper

with my father.

It's great to be underneath—

under the
laundry basket,

*Isn't this fun,
Thomas?*

under the laundry,

under the jackets on the coatrack,

and under the rug
in the hall.

WHERE'S NATALIE?
WHERE IS
THAT GIRL?

hee
hee
hee

Outside there are lots of
underneath places—

under our turtle,

under the board
where the ants live,

and under
the porch steps
with the spiders.

I like sitting
under
the umbrella

and having lunch
under
the lilac bush.

*Eat that nice
mud pie, Thomas.*

CHOC-CHIP

Under the sprinkler
is terrific.

Underneath the car,
even when it's stopped,
is not a good place

except
for
cats
and
sparrows,

but under the hood
with all the tubes and wheels
is fine, if it's with my father.

Being underneath is even nice
at nap time, except that sometimes,

underneath
his blanket,

underneath me,

Thomas yells a little.

Then my father says, "Natalie,
it's your turn to be underneath."

LET'S TAKE TURNS, NATALIE.

Supper is great
for being underneath—

under
the hamburger,

under
the
french
fries,

under the plate
where the writing is,

under
the napkins,

and under the sink,
helping my father
wash the dishes.

When we take our baths,
being underneath is lovely—
under the water,

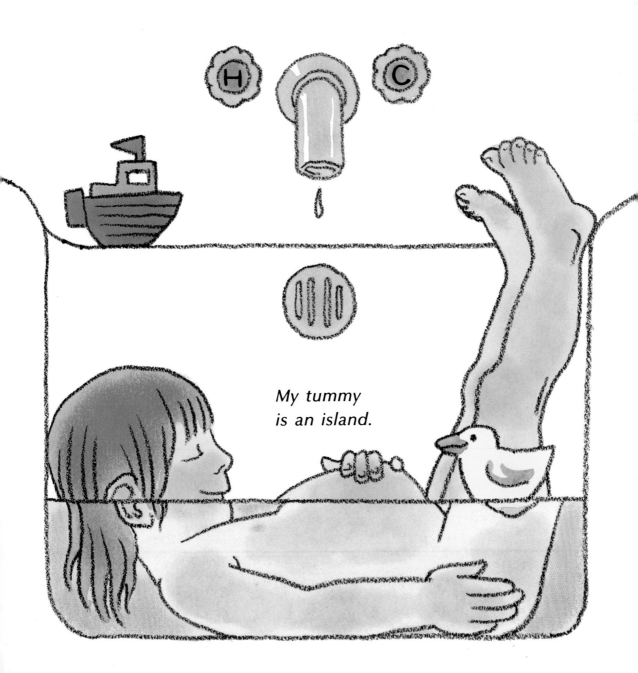

*My tummy
is an island.*

under the boats and ducks,
under the towels,

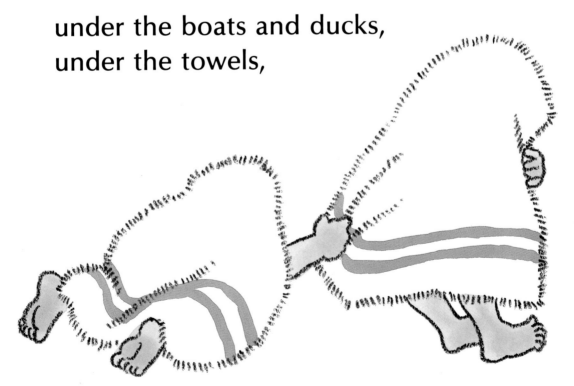

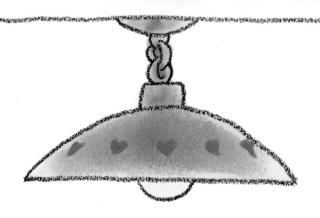

and under the ceiling,
which is too far away
to feel like underneath,

Being underneath at bedtime
is tremendous—
under the blankets,

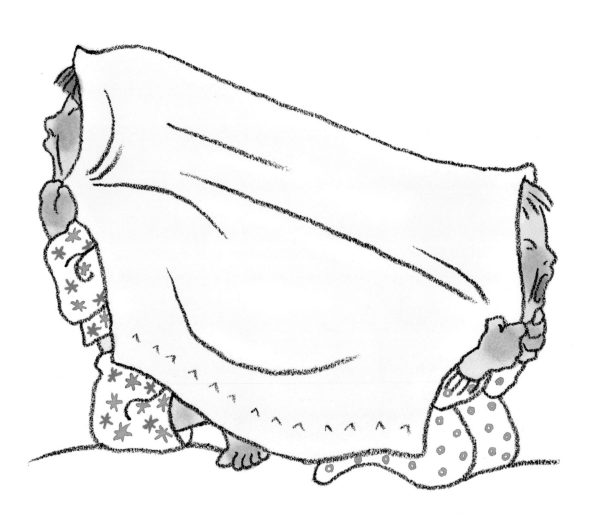

but never under the bed
because there are monsters there,
no matter what my father says.

But right before we go to sleep
is the best time to be underneath.

PORTVILLE FREE LIBRARY
Portville, New York 14770

*Good night,
you monsters.*

My father thinks so, too.

*Good night,
Thomas!*